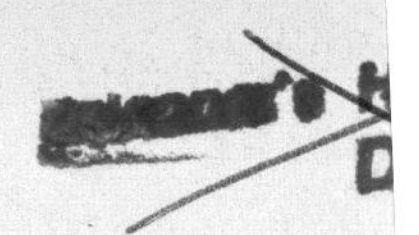

# Belinda
## Beats the Band

When Bert joins William Whisker's garage, he soon makes friends with Belinda, the little red Volkswagen Beetle. But then Bert is kidnapped – it's up to Belinda and her friends Susan and John to find him.

**Also by the same author,**
**and available in Knight Books:**

BELINDA THE BEETLE

# Belinda Beats the Band

REV W AWDRY

---

Illustrated by Val Biro

KNIGHT BOOKS
Hodder and Stoughton

First published in Great Britain in hardback in 1961 by Brockhampton Press Ltd

*Knight Books edition 1992*

**British Library CIP**

A Catalogue record for this book is available from the British Library

ISBN 0-340-58007-0

*The characters and situations in this book are entirely imaginary and bear no relation to any real person or actual happenings.*



Printed and bound in Great Britain for Hodder and Stoughton Children's Books a division of Hodder and Stoughton Ltd., Mill Road, Dunton Green, Sevenoaks, Kent TN13 2YA. (Editorial Office: 47 Bedford Square, London WC1B 3DP) by Clays Ltd, St Ives plc. Typeset by Rowland Phototypesetting Ltd., Bury St Edmunds, Suffolk.

# Contents

# 1 Ditched

The lorry swerved, bumping on the grass verge, then swung back to the road. The driver mopped his face.

'That was a near thing,' he exclaimed. 'Lucky that car was red or I wouldn't have seen it in time. We're O.K. – that's all that matters.'

His companion looked back.

'But they're not,' he protested. 'They're in the ditch. Stop, Jake! We must help them.'

'No fear,' muttered Jake. 'We've got no time. We're late now, and if we don't deliver the stuff on time the Boss will kill us.'

'But there were children,' urged the young man. 'I saw them. This is a lonely road. They might lie there hurt for hours. You can't do that to children, Jake. I've got a kid brother and sister just like them.' He opened the door and stood on the step. 'I'm going to jump off and go back.'

'Don't be a young fool, Bert. Come in and shut that door.' But when he saw that Bert was determined, he grudgingly stopped the lorry. 'You always were soft,' he said. 'Go and see if you must. We might get help sent; but we can't stop now.'

Bert crept behind the hedge as quickly as he could. He saw two children scramble out of the little red car, and help their father who had got

entangled in a bush. 'They're all right,' he said to himself. 'Thank goodness for that. They look like nice kids too.'

The children hurried down the road, talking as they came.

'They're going for help,' Bert thought. 'They mustn't see the lorry,' and he ran back across the field. But when he reached the place, the lorry had gone.

'That's that,' said Bert to himself. 'I'm not really sorry.' He wondered if he ought to go back to the car and offer to help; but he felt awkward about that, because he might say something to give away Jake's and his share in the accident. He didn't like Jake now. Jake didn't care about anybody except himself. But Jake *had* been kind to him and Bert thought it would be mean to give him away. He waited till the children were well ahead, and then walked after them himself.

The two children hurried down the road. The little boy looked despairingly at his sister as she strode away on her long legs.

'Wait for me, Susan!' he called.

'We can't wait, John. You must hurry.'

'How can I hurry?' panted the little boy. 'I've got a stitch.'

'Bother your stitches,' said his unsympathetic sister. 'You're always getting them.'

'I'm not.'

'You are.'

'I'm not.'

'Well anyway,' said Susan, 'you always seem to get them when we have to hurry. I bet you only pretend, so's I have to wait for you like I'm doing now.'

'I don't pretend,' said John indignantly. 'Mummy says I'm braver than you when I hurt myself.'

Susan knew this was true, and she was rather ashamed of it; but she wasn't going to admit it.

'Anyway,' she argued, 'I'm bigger than you, so my pains must be bigger than yours. So I feel them more.'

'How do you know?' countered John. 'You can't feel my feels.'

'Oh do come on!' said Susan, 'we shall never get to the telephone in time, and Mr Whisker will have left the garage, and poor Belinda will have to stay in the ditch all night.'

This was a sobering thought, and the children saved their breath for their travels.

Susan was a round-faced, cheerful little girl of ten. Her brother John was eight. He was smaller, slower, and dreamier than Susan. The children were very fond of each other indeed. Susan did her best to boss John; but he never let her do that if he could help it. This led to endless arguments, which were the despair of their parents. Their father was the Vicar of Arlstead, a small country town, and not long ago the family had bought a little red Volkswagen Beetle called Belinda. Belinda was the children's pride and joy.

At last they saw a huddle of houses. Susan pointed to the telephone box.

'There it is, John,' she said. 'Come on!'

Poor John's short legs could not keep up with Susan's long ones and he was left far behind. But Susan gained nothing by her haste, and she had to wait, almost dancing with impatience till John came up. John was carrying the coins their father had given them for the telephone.

'You have been an age, John. Mr Whisker's sure to have gone,' said Susan.

John refused to be hurried. He felt in his pocket and brought out a piece of wood, a lump of plasticine, two marbles, three toffees in a paper bag, and finally a very grubby handkerchief. He put everything else back in his pocket and then began to undo the knot in his hanky which contained the money.

'Buck up, do!' fumed Susan.

'Daddy said Mr Whisker shuts up shop at six o'clock,' he remarked placidly.

'Well,' said Susan, 'it's past six now, sure to be.'

'No, it isn't then,' said John triumphantly. 'Look at the church clock; it's only a quarter to.'

Susan calmed down, and the coins were laid ready. They found the number in the book, and then had an argument about who was to talk to Mr Whisker at the garage. When it came to the point, however, this was settled easily because John was not tall enough to reach the receiver properly.

'Mr Whisker,' said Susan. 'Oh, Mr Whisker, are you there?'

'Yes,' said Mr Whisker from the other end. 'This is Whisker's Garage. Who's speaking please?'

'Oh, Mr Whisker, it's me, Susan. Belinda's in a ditch, and Daddy can't get her out. We tried and tried ever so. A big lorry rushed along the middle of the road, and Belinda doesn't like lorries, so she swerved on to the grass, and fell in the ditch, and we can't get her out, and she looks so upset.'

'Good gracious, Susan, are you all right?' asked Mr Whisker.

'Oh yes,' said Susan. 'John and I scrambled out at the back. Daddy got stuck in a bush, and we had to help him wriggle out. His face is all scratches, but, Mr Whisker, it's Belinda. She's in the ditch all upset, and if she stays there much longer she'll be upsetter, and when she's upset she's cross and won't go. Please, Mr Whisker, will you ask George to come and pull her out?'

'I'll do better than that,' said Mr Whisker. 'I'll shut up shop and we'll both come. It's nearly closing time, anyway. You run back and tell your father we're coming. Where did you say you were?' Susan told him. 'By the way, Susan, does your mother know what's happened?'

'No, Mr Whisker. I can't tell her. I haven't any more money.'

'Never mind, I'll tell her. You go back to Belinda. We'll be along almost as soon as you.'

'Oh, thank you, Mr Whisker,' said Susan, and rang off.

The two children came to where their father was standing by the car. They told him what Mr Whisker had said. 'Thank you, pets,' he said. 'I hope George and William come in the rescue truck. They'll need tackle to get Belinda out of this.'

Belinda was looking sorry for herself. She was tilted up sideways and one of her front wheels was wedged in a ditch. The Vicar had been trying to lift her out, but the wheel had got wedged in a tree root. He had tried hard to hack it away with a pocket-knife. He had cut himself and blistered his hands, but had made no difference to the root. Belinda's wheel was as firmly wedged as ever. She was most indignant.

'I don't know what the roads are coming to, Mr Exel,' she was saying, 'with lorries racing about as if they owned them all, and pushing respectable cars off. It isn't as if I were an ordinary car neither. I'm special.'

A thought struck her.

'Mr Exel,' she asked anxiously. 'Is my jewel all right?'

John scrambled down to the ditch.

'Yes, Belinda,' he said. 'It's muddy but it's quite all right. You haven't knocked it off or anything. You just wait a sec, Belinda; I'll get my hankie out and clean it for you. It's all over mud.'

He felt in his pocket for his handkerchief. That was grubby too; but he wetted it with spit and set to work.

'You just wait, Belinda,' he said between rubs. 'I'll make it as bright and shiny as it was when

Admiral Eldbridge gave it to you for taking care of the jewels.'

'Thank you, John,' said Belinda happily. 'I shouldn't like George to see me with my jewel dirty. He's very particular, George is.'

Soon there was a distant rumbling, and the rescue truck came round the corner.

'Is that a lorry?' asked Belinda anxiously.

John looked up from his polishing.

'No,' he said. 'It's George and Mr Whisker.'

'Good,' said Belinda. 'Now I'll soon be all right.'

George left Mr Whisker talking to the Vicar, and came to Belinda.

'Well, well, well!' he exclaimed. 'You are in a mess.'

'Please get me out, George. I don't like being sideways. It's not what I'm used to,' she said plaintively. 'It's so upsetting. I don't like being upset, I don't. These lorries!' she went on crossly. 'They shouldn't be allowed. One gave me my first accident, and now this one makes me fall in a ditch. Do you know what I'm going to do with the next one? I'm going to toot my horn at him, telling him to get out of my way, and I'm going to go straight for him and make him go in a ditch and see how he likes it. Nasty smelly dieselly things taking up all the road. I'll . . .'

'Look, Belinda,' warned George, 'I shouldn't

try bumping lorries if I were you. The Vicar wouldn't like it.'

'But, George,' argued Belinda, 'I tell you . . . '

'Come on now, Belinda, give over chattering, do! I've got to see how we can get you out.'

Belinda calmed down while George examined her front wheel. Then he set to work with a saw. It was an awkward job, and George complained to

Belinda that he was not the right shape for working upside-down under cars in ditches; but it was done at last, and Belinda's wheel was freed.

'Shall we need the crane, George?' asked Mr Whisker.

'No, William, I think we can manage without that,' and he lifted Belinda's bumper experimentally.

'Vicar,' said George, 'would you mind holding Belinda's back end to see that she doesn't slip into the ditch while we lift her front? Now, William, are you ready? One. Two. Three. Heave!'

Belinda was not a heavy car, and once the root was cut away, the two men could lift her out of the ditch quite easily, so that she stood once more on the side of the road.

'Thank you, George. Thank you, Mr Whisker,' she said politely. 'I do like to be right side up.'

'So do we all,' laughed George. 'Now I'll just make sure you've no parts broken, and clean you up.'

George cleared off earth and mud, helped by the children. John's hankie was a deep shade of brown by the time he had finished. Then George tested her engine.

'You're as right as a trivet, Belinda,' he said as he wiped his hands. 'If you bring her in tomorrow,

Vicar, I'll fix that mudguard for you. You're very lucky to get off so lightly. Did you see the lorry's number? Better let Ted have it, and see what the police can do about tracing it.'

'Good idea, George,' said the Vicar. 'Thank you for reminding me. I'll call and have a word with Ted at the police-station on my way home. Thank you both very much indeed. Come on, poppets, hop in. It'll be well past bedtime before we get home.'

Belinda's mudguard rattled truculently all the way. She was thinking about lorries.

## 2 Lucky Penny

Bert Middley was eighteen. His father had died two years before while Bert was at school, and he had had to leave early and start work to help his mother bring up his young brother and sister.

For two years he had had what seemed a good job away from home. Then his firm failed, and he and a hundred others were out of work. He had hung on for a week or so, and had just made up his mind to go home, when he met Jake in a cheap café, and Jake had asked him to be driver's mate on his lorry. The work was simple, and the pay good, much better than he had any prospect of getting if he went home.

That was three months ago. All they had to do was to carry loads wherever they were ordered.

But there was a lot of secrecy and mystery about it, and Bert didn't like that. They worked mainly at night (today's daylight load had been an exception), and the loads had to be fetched from lonely places on dark nights. Quite often they had to go to country churchyards.

Bert could not understand that. He wondered what they were putting on the lorry. He asked Jake about it. But Jake shut him up at once. They were not allowed to ask questions, he said. All they had to do was to obey orders. They had these from the Boss who called himself the Bandmaster. Bert was more and more convinced that they were up to no good; but he was an easy-going, good-natured boy, and though he wanted to break away he didn't know how. He didn't want to hurt Jake's feelings.

Now all that was changed. Jake was cruel. He hadn't got any feelings. He'd caused an accident and then driven on. Besides, Jake had left him behind. Bert felt happier than he had been for weeks.

'I'm free of the Band at last,' he told himself. He strode along the road after the children, whistling cheerfully.

He had a few pounds in his pocket. That would be enough to get himself something for supper tonight, and breakfast tomorrow, leaving a little over for emergencies. After that – well, he was handy with cars, it was the week before August Bank Holiday, so he would surely be able to get a job in a garage for the busy time, and meanwhile he could send some money home and look out for another job.

He bought some bread and cheese in the village shop while the children were telephoning, and then walked on. That night he slept under a haystack, and finished his bread and cheese for breakfast next morning. Then he washed and tidied himself as best he could in a stream, and walked on again, whistling. This part of the

country was new to him. He didn't know where he was going and he didn't much care.

He came to a crossroads, and had a choice of three ways: left to Castle Dredcar, straight on to Arlstead, and right to Urlsburgh.

'Which way now?' he wondered. He took out a penny and tossed. Bert still has that penny, and he says he will never spend it. He calls it his 'luck'. It led him to Arlstead, to the best friends he has ever had, and it led him slap-bang into the most exciting adventure of his life.

## 3 Bert's new job

George Egg unlocked the door of his repair shop. He looked at all the cars waiting to be mended, and he sighed.

Mr Whisker came through from the show-room.

'My sainted aunt, George,' he exclaimed. 'How are we going to deal with all that lot?'

'Goodness knows,' answered George. 'You know, William, they seem to do it on purpose. They all bring their cars to us a few days before Bank Holiday, and they all want them mended by yesterday. It's disheartening, William. I have to rush everything, and I haven't time to do a good job on any of them.'

'Cheer up, George. We've had no complaints.

Everybody knows you're the best car doctor in Arlstead.'

'Maybe,' said George darkly, 'but not for long. When I went home last night I was worn to a shadow.'

William punched his sixteen-stone partner on the chest and grinned. 'Rubbish, George! You feel solid enough to me.'

'Ah!' said George. 'That's what supper and a good night's rest will do for a man. You wait till this evening. You'll come in here to see me about something, and you won't see me. You'll walk right through me! But seriously, William,' he went on, 'we're not as young as we were, and we've got more business than we can manage. What do you say to ringing up the Job Centre and getting someone in here to help us?'

'Right, George, I will,' and Mr Whisker went through, intending to telephone from the office at once; but he never did. A young man stood in the doorway looking about him shyly.

'Excuse me,' he said. 'Are you Mr Whisker?'

'Yes.'

'My name's Bert Middley,' said the young man, 'and I was wondering . . . that is I hoped . . . that you might be able to give me a job.'

Mr Whisker looked him up and down. His clothes were crumpled. His face was not as clean as it might be; but his eyes were clear and honest. Mr Whisker liked his looks.

'We do need an extra hand here,' he said slowly, 'but I'm not sure that you would suit. Have you done this sort of work before?'

'Oh yes, sir!' answered Bert eagerly. 'I was on maintenance at Selham's in Dredcaster, but they went bust, and I was out of a job. They gave me a reference, sir. Here it is,' and he pulled a crumpled envelope out of his pocket.

'H'm,' said Mr Whisker. 'It sounds all right . . .

"Apprentice here two years . . . good worker . . . promise of good mechanical aptitude". I see it's dated 17th April, and it's August now. What have you been doing since then?'

'I was driver's mate on a lorry, sir,' said Bert.

'What firm?' asked Mr Whisker.

Bert hesitated for a moment wondering what he had better say. 'It wasn't a firm, sir. It was a man who owned his own lorry. We used to pick up loads and deliver them where ordered.'

He looked a little uncomfortable, and Mr Whisker wondered why.

'Well,' he smiled, 'there's nothing wrong with that. Who was it?'

'It was a man who lived in Dredcaster, sir.'

'Go on,' urged Mr Whisker. 'What was his name? Perhaps we could write and get a reference from him too.'

Mr Whisker was still more puzzled at the look of dismay on Bert's face.

'If you don't mind, sir,' he stammered, 'I know it looks bad . . . but you see, sir . . . I wouldn't like . . . I'd rather not have a reference from him.'

'Oh!' said Mr Whisker. 'Why not? Did he sack you?'

'No, sir, I left him yesterday,' said Bert firmly.

'You left him! Why?'

'Well, you see, sir, I – I – I – didn't like something he did.'

'Why? What was wrong?'

'I'd rather not say, sir. You see, sir, though I don't want to have anything more to do with him, he did do me a good turn when I was out of work, and I shouldn't like to get him into trouble.'

'Like that, was it?' said Mr Whisker thoughtfully. 'He did something you thought was wrong, so you left him. I admire you for that. Come into the repair shop, and see my partner, George Egg.'

George looked up as they came through.

'That's quick work, William,' he said. 'I didn't think the Job Centre worked as fast as that!'

'I didn't telephone after all,' Mr Whisker told him. 'This young man was standing on the doorstep. He wants a job, so I've brought him in to see if you think he'll do. Here's his reference.'

George took it and read it slowly. Then he looked up and smiled at Bert.

'I see it's signed J. Upshott. Was his name Jim by any chance?'

'I think so, sir.'

'Well,' said George, 'if this is the Jim Upshott I knew, and he gives you a reference like this, we'd be fools not to give you a trial. I knew Jim well. He's a first-class mechanic. Was your Mr Upshott a big man?'

'Not as big as you, sir; but big enough. He played full-back in our works team.'

'That's the chap,' said George. 'I used to play too when I had a waistline. I vote we take Bert on for a fortnight. Then if we like him and he likes us we might think about something more permanent.'

'Agreed, George,' said Mr Whisker. 'Does that suit you, Bert?'

'It's better than I dared to hope, sir. Thank you both very much. Can I start at once?'

William saw the look of eagerness on his face and smiled.

'Presently,' he said. 'But we've got to register you at the Job Centre first. Come on. I'll give you a note and you can go round there at once.'

Half an hour later, Bert was at work with George when the Vicar brought Belinda.

'Here she is, George,' he said. 'There's not much the matter that I can see; but she's cranky and very sorry for herself. I know you're busy, but if you could get her ready for me to use on Sunday I'd be grateful.'

'Don't you worry, Vicar,' smiled George. 'I know how you're fixed. We'll have her ready by Saturday afternoon. Bert will bring her round for you at lunch-time.'

'Bert?' said the Vicar. 'I don't think I know Bert. He's new, isn't he?'

'Yes, sir, he came this morning,' said George.

The Vicar went to speak to Bert. Bert was glad

to see that he was none the worse for the accident.

'Good morning, Bert,' said the Vicar. 'So you've come to help George here. George is a good sort and you'll learn a lot. Anything that George doesn't know about cars isn't worth knowing.'

'I want to learn, sir. I love cars too,' Bert said.

'Then you and George should get on well. By the way, what's your surname?'

'Middley, sir.'

'Middley? Middley? I don't know any Middleys here. Are you a newcomer?'

'Yes, sir.'

'Have you any lodgings yet?'

'No, sir, I was going to try and find some in the dinner-break.'

'Try Mrs Warmly in Church Close. You tell her I sent you, and she'll do you proud.'

'Thank you, sir, I will.'

'Splendid! I'll be off then. Goodbye, George. Goodbye, Bert.'

Bert stood looking after him. 'You know, Geo . . . sorry, Mr Egg . . . '

'Go on, call me George. Everybody does.'

'You know, George, what I can't understand is, here am I a stranger and yet you're all so kind to me. You, Mr Whisker, the Vicar. Why?'

'Oh well,' said George gruffly, 'it's . . . it's . . . Oh get on with your work, lad, and don't ask silly questions.' So they left it at that.

## 4 Special delivery

Bert returned to work happily that afternoon. Mrs Warmly had given him a good welcome. She insisted on giving him dinner there and then, and made him feel at home at once.

George had promised to let him knock out the dents in Belinda's mudguard. He found George arguing with Belinda. Belinda was cross. She wanted George to mend her and no one else.

'Bert is new,' she kept saying. 'He doesn't know anything about me. I'm sure he'll put me back together wrong. He doesn't know where my parts go.'

'Oh yes he does, Belinda. Bert knows a lot about cars.'

'But does he know about ME?'

'Of course he does, Belinda. There are lots of cars like you.'

'No, he doesn't then,' said Belinda huffily. 'I'm a special car with a jewel. Bert's never seen a car with a jewel. Now has he?'

'He's never seen a car so conceited as you,' laughed George. 'Look here, Belinda. If you don't take care and behave, I'll ask the Vicar to take your jewel away till you're a better car.'

'Oh, George!' said Belinda dismayed. 'You wouldn't do that really, would you?'

'I would and all,' said George firmly, 'so behave yourself!'

George gave Bert a wink. Bert said, 'You've got a nice jewel there, Belinda. Tell me about it, please.'

So Belinda told him all about it, and she made it into a very long and complicated story. While she was telling it George slipped away, and Bert took her to pieces, mended her and put her together again. He tightened the last bolt just before she had finished.

'I like you, Bert,' she announced suddenly. 'You can mend me now.'

Bert chuckled.

'Do you know, Belinda,' he said, 'I've mended you already. All you need now is some paint, and we'll soon do that.'

There was silence while Belinda absorbed this

surprising news. 'Do you really mean,' she said at last, 'that while I was telling you all about my jewel and how brave I was and everything, you took me to pieces and mended me?'

'Yes,' said Bert, hiding a smile, 'I do.'

'Well for evermore!' exclaimed Belinda. She shook herself gently. 'Yes, I do believe you really truly mended me. I don't rattle like I used to.' She laughed delightedly. 'I can play tricks; but I didn't think that you could play tricks too. Do you know, Bert, I think you're clever. P'raps not so clever as George,' she went on candidly, 'but nearly. I shan't mind you mending me ever.'

Bert finished Belinda, and between them he and George managed to mend a surprising number of the other cars. By the time they stopped work at dinner-time on Saturday, he felt he had done a good job of work. George thought that too and said so. Bert took Belinda to the Vicarage, and whistled cheerfully as he walked back to Mrs Warmly's for his dinner. He turned a corner, and stopped dead. He was face to face with Jake.

'Hullo, Bert! I'd been hoping to meet up with you.' Jake looked round to make sure that no one was near. 'We're wanted for a job,' he whispered. 'Wednesday at eight. The Burnt Mill.'

'I'm not coming,' said Bert.

'Not coming?' said Jake, astonished.

'That's right,' said Bert. 'I've had enough. I

don't like this secret business. I'm sure it's not honest. I've decided to finish with it,' and he turned away.

Jake caught his arm. 'No you don't,' he hissed. 'You've not finished with us till we've finished with you. You be where I said and when I said, or else . . . ' Then he walked away.

Poor Bert had no appetite for dinner. Mrs Warmly was quite concerned about it.

Next week he worked well enough at the garage; but he was nervous and jumpy. One day Jake came in wanting something. Bert ducked down at once, and if Jake saw him he gave no sign. George attended to Jake who went away quite soon. Wednesday came and went; another week passed and nothing happened. Bert began to feel a little easier.

'Perhaps they'll leave me alone,' he thought hopefully. 'Now that I've shown I don't want to have any more to do with them.'

That afternoon he was doing a job he enjoyed; tuning up a powerful car. It had come in the day before and was wanted urgently that evening. It belonged to a Mr Redgold who gave as his address a big house called Lone Tower, on the Castle Dredcar Road. Neither George nor Bert had met him before; but he explained that he was a newcomer and had taken the house a day or two ago.

Naturally anxious to oblige a new customer, Bert had agreed to deliver the car himself as soon as it was ready. He told George and drove away. He went slowly through the town, and was delighted to find that the car ran well. He soon reached Mr Redgold's house, and the car crunched along the gravel to the front door. He sprang out and rang the bell. It was answered by a maid in uniform. She looked as if she had put it on very hurriedly.

'Whisker's Garage, miss,' said Bert. 'I've brought Mr Redgold's car.'

'Mr Redgold's out now,' said the maid in a curiously deep voice, 'but he wants to see you most particularly: he said for me to ask you to wait.'

'Certainly,' said Bert, and he turned back to wait in the car.

'Mr Redgold said would you wait inside.'

'I don't mind if I do,' answered Bert and followed her unsuspectingly into the house.

The maid led him to a room at the back. Bert thought this a little strange, but did not take much notice. The windows were barred, and looked out on an untidy laurel hedge. The room had been used as a gun-room, and there were racks on the walls and some rather faded sporting prints. The only furniture was a table and an old-fashioned leather armchair.

'Make yourself at home,' said the maid in her deep voice. 'Mr Redgold will be back at half-past six.' She went out and the door clicked sharply behind her.

Bert sat down gratefully. He enjoyed the coolness of the room. He began to think about his own affairs. 'My fortnight's nearly up. I wonder if George and Mr Whisker will want to keep me on. I hope they do. I like working with old George. If only I could be sure that Jake would let me alone, I'd do fine. Why shouldn't I leave Jake if I want to? He's got no right to threaten me like that. I've done nothing wrong.'

He jumped up. 'Of course! What a fool I am! Why should I try and protect Jake when all the time he's threatening me? I could stop him if I liked. I've done nothing wrong. I'll tell Mr Whisker about it tomorrow. He'll understand and tell me what to do.'

He looked through the window.

'It's getting quite dark. It must be long past half-past six.' He listened. 'This house is very quiet. I wonder if he's forgotten me and gone out again.'

He tried to open the door and found it locked. 'That's funny! Perhaps the maid locked it by

mistake. She did look a bit odd. She had an odd voice too for a girl, more like a man.'

He hammered on the door. 'Let me out! Let me out!' he shouted. For a long time nothing happened, so he kept on hammering and shouting. Then he heard footsteps.

'All right, all right, young fellow, I'm coming,' said a voice.

The key turned, the door opened. Bert stepped forward eagerly.

'I'm sorry, Mr Redgold,' he said. 'I'm sure there's been a mista . . .'

His heart gave a thump and he started backwards. It wasn't Mr Redgold. It was Jake.

# 5 Holiday morning

The sun peeped through the curtains, tickled Susan's nose and danced lightly over her face. She woke, yawned, stretched, and lay watching the pools of light chase each other over the ceiling. She felt excited, but couldn't quite remember why.

Suddenly she knew. She shot out of bed and danced down the passage to John's room. She bounced on his bed.

'John, you slug! Wake up!'

John turned over, and snuggled under the bedclothes. 'I'm not a slug,' he protested sleepily, 'and I won't wake up.'

'Yes, you are a slug,' said his sister severely, 'a great big fat slug like we found under the lettuces yesterday. Look at me,' she went on virtuously, 'I've been awake for ages and ages.'

'I won't look at you,' came from under the bedclothes, 'and I bet you haven't been awake for ages and ages.'

'Well,' said Susan, 'p'raps not quite ages and ages; but anyway I've been awake for ten whole minutes and that's ages on a day like this; and if that doesn't show what a slug you are, I don't know what will,' and she bounced him again and again.

'John,' she said in between bounces, 'do – you – know – what – day – it – is?'

'It's – Thurs – day. Do – stop – boun – cing, – Sus – an; it – makes – me – ad – dled.'

Susan stopped, exhausted. 'No, silly! I don't mean that sort of what day is it. I mean what special day is it?'

John pushed the bed-clothes away and looked at Susan. Then he saw an open suitcase on the floor.

'I know,' he said. 'It's the day we go away.'

The two children sat side by side in the middle of the bed where it was springiest. 'It's the day' – bounce bounce – 'we go away' – bounce bounce. The bed creaked and groaned. There was a thumping from the next room.

'Oh dear!' said Susan. 'Mummy and Daddy have woken up.' They padded into their parents' room. 'Did we wake you up?' she asked innocently.

'Yes, you did,' groaned Daddy. 'Come here, you miserable specimens, and be spiflicated.' Susan approached her father's bed cautiously, and sat on the end keeping a wary eye on his clutching fingers. She grinned at him. 'Do you know what day it is, Daddy?'

'Come hither,' hissed Daddy, 'and I'll whisper.'

Susan wriggled delightedly. 'You can't catch me, Daddy.'

'No,' said Mummy. 'Because you and John are going to go downstairs, and make some tea for us. But put on your dressing gowns and slippers first.'

The two grown-ups lay quietly talking over all the things that still needed to be done before they could start. They were exchanging parishes for the holiday with the Vicar of Tinwell, and as they were going to live in his house and he and his family were going to live in theirs, they were anxious to leave everything just so. Mrs Exel looked at the clock.

'Those two are a long time,' she said. 'I suppose I'd better get up and see what's happening.'

'Never fear, Mummy dear, here they come,' and the Vicar grinned at his wife. The sound of argument came nearer and nearer, accompanied by the clinking of crockery. Outside the door the children stopped and disputed hotly each other's right to give Daddy and Mummy their tea.

'Buck up, for goodness' sake,' called Mummy, and the door swung open revealing John resisting Susan's attempt to take the tray from him. He carried it in triumphantly and balanced it precariously on a chair. Susan poured out the tea.

'Thank you, pets,' said Mummy. 'That was lovely. Now Daddy and I are going to get up. We've lots to do before breakfast. Put on your oldest clothes and go and polish Belinda. You haven't done her for ages, and she's rather put out about it. Off you go!'

By half-past nine, as a result of all this early rising, Belinda stood at the front door pleased and shining. The children, even by Mummy's exacting standards, were clean and tidy. All the last-minute jobs had been done, and the Exel family were ready to start.

'Well I never did!' said Mummy. 'Ready on time. That's a record for this family. Come on, Daddy, let's go before something happens to delay us.'

Daddy turned the key. Belinda purred happily. 'I think we've settled everything,' said Mr Exel. 'What could happen, Mummy old dear?'

But something nearly did.

They called at the garage for some petrol. Mr Whisker put in too much and some over-flowed.

'Sorry, Vicar,' he said, 'I was daydreaming.'

'What's the matter, William?'

Mr Whisker replaced the filler cap.

'We've had a tremendous hoo-ha here this morning. First of all Bert never came to work. Then Mrs Warmly arrived wanting to know where he was. She said he hadn't been home all night. So I rang up the police and they came here and heard her story, and now they're both at Lone Tower looking round.'

'Lone Tower! That's the house on the Castle Dredcar Road,' said the Vicar. 'Why on earth have they gone there?'

'Because Bert was last seen taking a car there,' replied Mr Whisker.

'But it's empty. There's a board up.'

'That's what I thought; but a man came in the day before yesterday giving the name of Redgold. He said he had just taken Lone Tower and he wanted his car repaired. He wanted it urgently yesterday evening, and asked if Bert could deliver it personally. Bert's done that sort of thing quite a bit since he came, so we didn't think twice about it. I saw him drive away, and no one's seen him since. I'm disappointed with Bert. I didn't think he'd run out on us. He seemed a nice lad and getting on well.'

'I don't think Bert's the sort to let you down, William. I'm sure there's some good explanation. You just wait and see. I can't stop now, the family's waiting, but do let me know what happens.'

Back in Belinda the others peppered him with questions, and he told them all he knew.

'We'll go along the Castle Dredcar Road,' he said, 'and stop at Lone Tower. Perhaps the police will tell us something.'

# 6 At Lone Tower

Constable Keenan stood in the driveway and began to wave them away. Then he recognised Belinda.

'Sorry, Vicar,' he said. 'You haven't got your collar on and I thought you were one of these reporters. You'll want to see the sergeant, I expect. He's in the house looking round. It's a strange set-up, and no mistake. The hall's furnished just as if the house was lived in. There's lino, hats, coats, pictures, barometer, and even a vase of flowers on a table. But there's no furniture at all in any of the other rooms except two. One's the kitchen, where there's some chairs and a table, and the remains of some sort of meal. The sergeant's looking at the other room. Here it is.'

He opened the door. 'The Vicar to see you, Sergeant,' he announced.

'Good morning, Ted,' said the Vicar. 'I'm sorry to butt in, but I'm interested in Bert, as you know, and we're leaving for our holiday today and I want to know as much as I can before we go.'

The sergeant turned from the window and greeted the family. 'We can't say yet what's happened to young Middley, Vicar; but there are some interesting things here. This window now, one of the bars has been wrenched right out, and the window's been left swinging open. Then look at the door. The lock has been oiled and there are

bolts on the outside, newly put on by the look of them.'

'Someone has been locked in here, but pulled out one of the bars and escaped through the window.'

'That's about it, Vicar,' said the sergeant.

'Was it Bert who was locked up and escaped?' asked Susan. 'I'm so glad.'

'Yes, Susan, it might have been Bert. We don't know for certain, but it is very likely. Those things on the table will tell us. Don't touch, please.' This last remark was necessary because the children went to the table at once. 'There's a handkerchief, a broken knife blade, and a pocket screwdriver badly bent. The handkerchief has A.M. on it. That might stand for Albert Middley. We'll have to ask Mrs Warmly about that. We found it on the floor wrapped round the bar.'

'Why was it round the bar, sergeant?'

'I expect he twisted it round to protect his hands, John. Otherwise he'd have got blisters from pulling at it.'

'The knife blade,' went on the sergeant, 'was stuck in the wood of the window. Obviously he was digging away with it when it broke and he had to use his screwdriver instead. It's very badly bent, as you see.'

John gazed at the screwdriver with interest. 'I'm sure that's Bert's,' he said. 'I saw him mend

Belinda with it. It's got a yellow handle you can see through.'

'I expect you're right, John,' smiled the sergeant, 'but those screwdrivers are very common. I've got one myself. You can get them at Woolworth's any time you like. We'll have to compare the fingerprints on these things with those on Bert's tools at the garage. Then we can be sure. Anyway, whoever it was got away through the window, and, judging by the mess outside, he was chased all over the garden.'

'Poor boy!' said Mummy. 'I hope he escaped.'

'As to that, Mrs Exel, we can't say yet; but I don't think it likely.'

'Why not, Sergeant?'

'If young Middley really was here, and if he did escape, he'd come back to his friends. He knew that you, Vicar, and George, and William Whisker, and Mrs Warmly would help him, even if he did feel shy about coming to us. Still it's early yet. He may be hiding till the coast's clear. Anyway, Vicar, don't worry, we'll find him.'

'I'm sure you will, Ted, and the best of luck. Thank you for telling us all this. We won't say a word about it to anyone. Goodbye,' and the vicarage family hurried away.

Once on the main road Daddy said, 'We came out of our way to call here, but if we turn right at the next crossroads we can cut across country.'

Mummy was thoughtful. 'I wonder if Bert was really shut up in that room.'

'It's very likely,' said Daddy. 'William Whisker says that Bert set out to deliver that car to Lone Tower. Now what would he do when he got there?'

'He'd drive the car up to the front door and ring the bell,' said Susan.

'Yes,' said Mummy, 'and then someone would come to the door, and Bert would see the hall furnished, and not suspect anything.'

'Then,' continued Daddy, 'they'd say perhaps that Mr Redgold wanted to see him to ask him something about the car, so would he come in.'

'They'd take him to the room all unsuspecting,' went on Susan, 'and they'd lock him in . . . '

' . . . and he cut away the wood and escaped out of the window,' finished John triumphantly.

'But why lock him up?' puzzled Daddy. 'That's what I can't understand.'

'Oh, I do wish we could find him,' said Susan. 'Wouldn't it be fun? I wish we could find some clues. Daddy, can't we stop and look?'

'No,' said Daddy firmly. 'We haven't time. Ah! here's the turning. But I tell you what. There's a nice place a few miles along here where I get out and rest sometimes. It's beautifully shady and cool. It's just the place for our elevenses. I could just do with some. I've almost forgotten what breakfast was like.'

'Good idea,' smiled Mummy. 'I'm as thirsty as anything.'

So presently they turned Belinda through an opening in the hedge, and parked her in the shade. The hedge was thick and she was quite hidden from the road. Mummy poured out drinks and handed round the biscuit tin. The children quickly finished theirs and ran off to explore.

'Don't go far, dears,' called Mummy. 'We will have to be starting again soon.'

The children soon came back looking excited.

'Daddy, Mummy,' said Susan, 'we went into the bushes a little way, and we came to a steep place and John nearly slipped, and I helped him up, and then we looked down where John nearly tumbled, and there was a man, and a hut, and a lorry, and the man looked as if he was doing secret things, and we suspected him, and we looked again, and John and I think it's the lorry that made Belinda fall in the ditch, because there's a splodge of green paint on it just like the other.'

Daddy was lying comfortably on his back and didn't feel at all inclined to get up.

'I wonder,' he said lazily, 'if it really is the same? There are lots of lorries about, you know, and I expect a good many of them have got paint sploshed on them.'

The children meanwhile were dancing with impatience and excitement.

'Daddy, do *please* come. We're sure it's the same,' begged John.

Daddy groaned, and got up.

'All right,' he said. 'I'll come; but we mustn't waste time. Mummy dear, would you put the things in the car so that we can start quickly when we get back?'

Daddy and the children crept quietly through the bushes to the edge of an old gravel pit. 'Bless me!' said Daddy. 'I've stopped here dozens of times, and didn't even know about this pit.'

'Sh! Daddy please. He'll hear you!' said Susan.

They peered over the edge, and saw the hut, and the man, and the lorry. The man came out of the hut carrying a heavy bundle. The bundle looked like a roll of carpet; but there was something funny about it. It seemed heavier and stiffer than a roll of carpet ought to be. The man found it hard to carry. He put it down twice on the way to the lorry, and each time he said something.

'That's funny,' whispered Susan. 'It's just as if he was talking to the carpet. I wish we could hear what he's saying.'

The man reached the lorry at last, put the bundle down carefully, and spoke again.

John had been silent all this time. He had been pondering deeply.

'I think,' he whispered at last, 'that he's got someone rolled up in that carpet.'

'I can't be sure you're right about the carpet, John,' said Daddy, 'but you're certainly right about the lorry. It's got the same number and everything. Come on, poppets, let's get down to Belinda, and see which way it goes. If it goes the way we want to go, we'll follow.'

# 7 The chase

Susan reached Belinda first.

'Belinda,' she panted, 'it's so exciting. There's a lorry and a man and a roll of carpet, and he put it in the lorry and we think it's Bert.'

'What! My Bert who mended me?' asked Belinda.

'Yes, and . . . '

'But my Bert's in the garage with George,' said Belinda.

'Oh,' said Susan, didn't you know he isn't? They're ever so worried about him. They don't know where he is. But,' she went on excitedly, 'John and I do. The man put a carpet in the lorry, and it's Bert.'

'Don't talk silly,' said Belinda severely. 'Bert's

Bert. He isn't a carpet. He couldn't be. It's not natural.'

'It's you that's silly,' Susan retorted. 'Bert isn't the carpet. He's rolled in the carpet.'

This was too much for Belinda to believe. 'Now what would my Bert want to roll in a carpet for, I should like to know? Bert wouldn't do anything so daft. My Bert's clever, he is. He can play tricks like me. He wouldn't be daft and roll in a carpet.'

'Oh, Belinda, can't you understand?' said John. 'Bert didn't roll in the carpet. The man rolled him up in the carpet, and put him in the lorry like a parcel, and,' went on John importantly, 'we think, Susan and I, that he's been kid – kid – kid . . . '

' . . . napped,' finished Susan. 'Don't you see, Belinda?'

'No, I don't,' snapped Belinda crossly. 'You're daft, both of you. Even if my Bert had been kid – whatever it was you said, he wouldn't be so silly as to roll in a carpet. I don't believe it. First you say my Bert's a carpet, then you say he rolls in carpets, and now you say he's a parcel. Stop talking, do. You've got me all muddled.'

'Oh dear!' sighed Susan. 'I wish Belinda would try to understand.'

'I rather sympathise with Belinda, Susan,' said Mummy. 'I find it rather muddling myself. Thank goodness, here's Daddy. Daddy dear, what is all this about the lorry, and the man, and Bert being a parcel in a carpet?'

Daddy laughed. 'I'm not surprised, my dear,' he said. 'I'm rather muddled myself. All I really know is that we looked over the edge of an old gravel pit, and saw a man putting a roll of carpet on to a lorry. It seemed too heavy and awkward to be an ordinary roll, and the childen think that there's someone inside it. Their guess is that it's Bert. They may be right, I wouldn't know, but I do know that the lorry is the very same one which sent us into the ditch.'

'Mr Exel,' said Belinda, 'did you say that that lorry's the lorry that pushed me into the ditch?'

'Yes, Belinda, it is. It's got the same number and everything. Sh! here it comes.'

They watched it rumble past their opening.

'That's it, Mr Exel,' said Belinda eagerly. 'Come on! What are we waiting for?'

The lorry was big, and though the lane twisted and turned, they could see it easily over the hedges. Belinda pounded along behind.

'Nasty, smelly, dieselly old lorry,' she said to herself. 'We'll catch you. Won't Mr Exel give you what for for pushing me in the ditch?'

They ran through villages, up and down hills, over bridges, always keeping the lorry in sight, but never coming too close. Belinda was enjoying herself hugely. That was of course till they reached the level-crossing. The lorry slipped through just before the gates were closed; but Belinda had to wait panting till the train had passed. She tooted impatiently.

'Hurry, Mr Gatekeeper, please!' The poor man did his best, but that wasn't quick enough for Belinda. Daddy tried to hold her back, but she jerked forward almost before the gates were open. The gatekeeper jumped back in surprise.

'Sorry, Mr Gatekeeper,' she panted. 'Got to see a lorry about a ditch.'

By this time the lorry was a long way ahead, and out of sight; but Belinda ran as fast as ever she could. Presently the children shouted, 'There it is, Belinda. Can you see it, Daddy?'

The lorry looked like an insect in the distance, crawling up the slope of a long, steep hill. The children cheered, Belinda tooted in her excitement. Daddy pressed hard on the accelerator, and Belinda flew up the hill like a bird, gaining on the lorry every minute. The lorry reached the top and disappeared. Belinda was not far behind, but this was the steepest bit of all.

'Oh, my gears and differential!' she groaned. 'I can't go any faster. Never mind, we'll see it again in a minute,' but Belinda could only crawl the last few hundred metres, and when she thankfully reached the top and trundled down the other side, the lorry had gone.

Four pairs of eyes scanned the road ahead.

'There it is,' called Susan.

'Where?'

'There.'

'No, silly, that's a tractor,' said John scornfully.

'Then where is it?' asked everybody. But nobody knew.

'It just couldn't vanish into thin air,' said Daddy. 'It must be somewhere. Look, the road

goes through a wood. We'll see it when it's clear of the trees.'

But they didn't. There was a crossroads in the wood. They stopped and looked to see which way it had gone; but the ground was hard and dry, and there were no tyre marks. The children were disappointed and Belinda was so upset that she nearly cried.

'Come on,' said Mummy at last, shepherding them back to the car. 'We can't waste time traipsing round the country after lorries. Tell the police about it, Daddy, if you must, and say where you

saw it last; but for goodness' sake let's get on and have our holiday in peace.'

'Mummy's right as usual,' said Daddy. 'Come on, all of you. We can't afford to hang about any longer if we're going to get there before dark.'

It was a sad and dispirited family and car that chugged away from the crossroads in the woods.

Jake on the other hand was highly delighted. He had watched the whole thing from behind a hedge.

'Given them the slip at last,' he crowed. 'Now we can get to Tinwell in peace. Grand place Tinwell for a hideout. No one would ever think of going to such an obscure hole!'

## 8 Mr Blueton is annoyed

Mr Blueton sat in his house at Tinwell. It was small, and all by itself in the fields near the church. He had bought it cheaply and had rebuilt it to suit himself. When people asked why he chose to bury himself in such a place, he said that he had retired from business, and needed privacy, peace and quiet.

He was not telling the truth. For one thing his real name was not Blueton, and for another he had not retired, but wanted to carry on his business undisturbed. The police would have been very interested in what kept him so busy.

Near the house was a field where there were some ruins. Cellars were under those ruins. Mr

Blueton had improved them without asking the owner's permission.

Mr Blueton was annoyed. He looked at his watch impatiently. He rang the bell. His manservant answered it.

'Spike,' he asked, 'hasn't Jake arrived *yet?*'

'No, sir.'

Mr Blueton tapped the arm of his chair. 'I can't understand it. I made the arrangements myself. The boy was to bring my car to Lone Tower on Wednesday. He was to be kidnapped there, and brought here in the car the same night. Now it's nearly midnight on Thursday. Why aren't they here?'

'Couldn't say, sir.'

'Incompetent, bungling fools!'

'Sir?'

'Not you! Them!' snapped Blueton. 'No car, no lorry. The police are getting interested in us. They don't know about this place yet; but unless that boy Middley is kept quiet, they soon will. We must get that cellar cleared. It should have been done tonight. We can do nothing at weekends with people about. Now we must wait till Monday night. Listen! That sounds like Jake. Bring him here at once.'

Jake came in, pushing Bert in front of him. Bert had to be guided, for Jake had blindfolded him. Spike closed the door and stood on guard.

'I am sorry, young man,' said Blueton smoothly, 'to have to inconvenience you by blindfolding; but I really cannot allow you the privilege of recognising me.'

Bert said nothing, but he remembered the voice. It was Redgold's.

Blueton turned to Jake. 'You're late,' he snapped. 'Why?'

'The plan went wrong, Bandmaster,' Jake cringed. 'Middley escaped, and we had to chase him in the dark. He put your car out of action and took to the road. I searched all night; but didn't find him till morning. I rolled him in a carpet to keep him quiet and avoid suspicion; but we were tailed, and I had to hide till they had gone.'

'Followed, were you? Who by?'

'By some people in a red car. We'd an accident with them a fortnight ago. They must have remembered the lorry. I shook them off though.'

'Fool!' hissed the Bandmaster. 'They'll have reported the lorry by now. Change the number. The spares are in the barn.'

Jake turned to go. 'Not now,' ordered the Bandmaster. 'Later.' He turned to Bert. 'Now, Middley, Jake says you want to leave the Band. Why is that?'

'I've finished,' said Bert boldly, but he didn't feel as brave as he sounded. 'It's not honest.'

'Oho!' chuckled the Bandmaster softly, 'so you've turned honest, have you? That really is most unfortunate – for you – ' He turned to the two men. 'Take him away. Put him in the new cellar. No rough stuff, mind. We'll keep him there till Tuesday. He may have changed his mind by then.' They turned to go. 'By the way, Spike, tell Tipper that though we can't prevent people from using the field as a short cut to the woods, he must at all costs discourage them from poking round the ruins.'

Earlier that same evening the Exel family had arrived at Tinwell Vicarage. Next morning at breakfast Susan said:

'This is a funny village, Daddy.'

'What makes you say that, pet?'

'It hasn't got a church. Me and John we looked through all the windows upstairs last night, and we couldn't see it anywhere.'

Daddy smiled. 'I'm not surprised, Susan. There is a church, but it's half a mile away behind some trees in a field. Mummy and I walked there last night after you two were in bed.'

'But why is it so far away?'

'Mummy asked that too. So when we got back we hunted in the study and found a book which told us about it. Once upon a time the houses were built round the church. It was quite a big village, and an old Roman road ran through it, bringing travellers and traders and pilgrims.'

'Pilgrims, Daddy? Why did they come?'

'They came to St Ina's well.'

The children repeated the name. At last light dawned. 'Daddy, is that why it's called Tinwell?'

'Yes.'

'Go on, Daddy, please. Why aren't the houses there now?'

'Because the people were frightened away. Listen! A long time ago doctors weren't so clever as they are now, and there were many illnesses they couldn't cure. The worst was one called the Black Death. When some people in the village caught it, the others got frightened. They ran away and built themselves new houses right away from the old village. But they couldn't pull down the church and build a new one. So that is why Tinwell people live so far away.'

'There is one house,' said Mummy, 'close to the church. Do you remember, Daddy? We saw the lighted windows through the trees.'

'Yes, and the book says that till about 110 years ago, the vicarage was there too. When the Black Death frightened people away, it didn't frighten the Vicar. He stayed, and looked after the sick people.'

'I think he was brave,' said Susan. 'I hope he didn't catch it.'

'That I don't know,' said Da
didn't say; but the Vicars of Tinwe
living in the house by the church till it wa
down. Then they built a new one here, close to t
people.'

## 9 Keep out

They left Belinda behind that afternoon and walked the half-mile to the church. The door was locked, and Daddy had forgotten to bring his key; but he promised that they should come with him tomorrow when he went to get ready for Sunday. Then they walked over the churchyard grass, and climbed the fence into the old vicarage field.

Both church and field were on a little hill in the middle of a valley. It was easy to see where the old house had been, because stone and brick showed in places through grass which had been close cropped by sheep.

Susan pointed over to the left. 'Is that the old house you were telling us about, Mummy? It doesn't look old, it looks new.'

'Yes,' said Mummy, 'it does look new, doesn't it? They were telling me about it in the village shop this morning. A Mr Blueton bought it about two years ago and he has rebuilt it very nicely. They don't like Mr Blueton, though. They say he interferes.'

Daddy laughed. 'I don't suppose he'll interfere with us. Look at that shepherd's hut by the gate. That's an old ruin if you like!'

The family set the picnic basket under a shady tree, and strolled over to the ruined house. The sheep, after their first surprise at strangers, settled down to graze quietly once more.

There wasn't very much to see, and the children amused themselves by playing hide-and-seek among the grassy hummocks of the ruins. Nobody noticed a man watching them from the door of the hut.

Tea-time soon came, and when it was all finished, Daddy suggested a walk to St Ina's well in the woods.

John looked at him anxiously. 'Do we *have* to go, Daddy?'

'No, of course not. Do you want to do anything special?'

'Yes, Daddy, please. Susan and me have found a special secret place, and we want to explore it.'

'Splendid!' said Daddy. 'Then Mummy and I can have a nice peaceful time keeping an eye on you.'

But parents' peace never lasts long! After a few minutes John came back looking red in the face.

'Daddy, Mummy, please come,' he panted. 'There's a sheep stuck in our special place and we can't get it out.'

They followed him across the field, and saw that the sheep was stuck in what looked like a narrow cleft among some bushes. Susan was hot and exasperated. 'The silly thing!' she exclaimed. 'It can't go forwards, and it *won't* go backwards. John and me, the more we try to pull it back, the more forwarder it goes and the stucker it gets.'

Daddy took charge of operations, and they went round in front and tried to shoo it from there. But that didn't help. The sheep was below them, and their shooings went over its head. It continued to bleat for help, but otherwise took no notice.

'This is no good,' said Daddy at last.

Then Mummy had a bright idea. 'Susan, John,' she said. 'Can you both squeeze down into the hole and stand at the sheep's head?'

'Splendid!' said Daddy. 'Mummy and I are too fat to get down there too, so we'll sit on the edge here and shoo.' Susan didn't much like the idea of getting close to the sheep's front end; but John had slithered down at once, and so, not to be outdone, she had to go too.

The sheep was already beginning to feel unnerved by the two children almost in front of its nose, and when the family all shooed together, it forgot that it couldn't go backwards, scooted out of the cleft, and ran bleating indignantly to its friends on the other side of the field.

The children were now free to explore. Daddy and Mummy sat together enjoying the sunshine and laughing at the sheep. Their attention was drawn by excited squeaks from the children. 'Look! There's some steps and a door. Is it a secret passage?'

'I'm sorry to disappoint you, pets,' said Daddy,

'but I think it's an outside door to the cellar of the old house. It's probably filthy dirty, anyway, because no one's been down there for years.' However, he slid down, and was surprised to find that though the steps were grass grown, the door was by no means the rotten relic that one would expect. When he tapped it with a stone it felt surprisingly solid. He began to lift the latch.

'Come out of that,' said a harsh voice behind them. 'You're trespassers, that's what you are. Trespassers will be persecuted.'

They turned and saw a man in a battered felt hat, a stained shirt and corduroy trousers, glaring at them.

'I'm sorry,' said Daddy. 'We got down here to help the sheep, and we saw this interesting door.'

'Never mind that door,' said the man truculently. 'You were a-scaring of my sheep. I saw you. Waving of your arms at it and shouting. You get out of this, see, or I'll have the law on you.'

'We didn't scare it,' said Susan indignantly. 'We were saving it.'

'That's quite true,' said Daddy quietly. 'Are you the shepherd?'

'Yes.'

'Then,' went on Daddy, 'you should take better care, and put hurdles to stop your sheep getting into dangerous places.'

'Look here, mister, there's no call for you to think you can teach me my job.'

'And,' said Daddy, 'there's no call for you to be so rude. We've done no harm to you or your sheep, and you can't prosecute unless we have. If we have any more rudeness I shall find out who your employer is and report you.'

The man's attitude changed. 'I beg your pardon, sir,' he said. 'I was anxious about your opening that there door. It's dangerous, see? You might get hurt.'

'Why?'

'I dunno, sir. Mr Blueton, that's the gentleman who lives yonder, he says to me: "Tipper," he says, "you take my tip and keep away from that door. It's dangerous." Take my advice, sir, and keep out.' He turned away and went to examine the sheep. He seemed disappointed to find it quite unhurt. Then he shambled over to the hut and slammed the door.

## 10 Explorers

After Service on Sunday morning, Mummy and the children stood under the tower waiting for Daddy to finish in the vestry. They were looking at an interesting stone in the floor. It was a large slab, about nine feet long and three feet wide. The brass set in it was worn with years of polishing. It showed a priest in full church robes (called vestments) lifting his right hand in blessing. Susan thought that his face looked kind but a little sad.

Just then, Daddy came out and introduced Mr Doman, farmer and churchwarden. 'I see you're looking at our old Vicar,' said Mr Doman. 'Brave man, he was. He stayed behind and looked after the people who had caught the plague. He caught

it himself in the end, poor chap. I've heard tell there's a mystery about this stone. An old chap in the village who died when I was a youngster said he'd seen the stone move; but why it should move I can't think. It sounds daft to me.'

'You never know,' said Daddy. 'These stories sound strange, but there's generally something behind them.'

He and Mummy stooped down and together spelt out the worn Latin words of the inscription. 'Nicholas. Priest. Died 1349.' Underneath was a text. 'I am the good shepherd.'

'Yes,' said Mr Doman, 'he was a good shepherd and no mistake.' They started to walk together towards the door. 'That reminds me, Vicar. Thank you for rescuing my sheep on Friday.'

'Then is it your field?' asked Mummy, 'and is that rude man your shepherd?'

'Yes. I'm sorry he was rude and tried to turn you off. You can go there and welcome, anytime you like. You needn't take notice of Tipper, or Blueton, or anyone else.'

'Thank you very much.'

'Good,' said the children excitedly, 'then we *can* go through that door, can't we, Daddy, please?'

Mr Doman looked puzzled, and Daddy explained.

'Do you know?' said the farmer, 'I've lived here all my life and I've never been down those cellars yet. You say the door was sound, Vicar, not rotten at all?'

'Yes, I was surprised.'

'It sounds to me as if those cellars must be good and dry.' Mr Doman suddenly had an idea. 'I've a good mind to look at them myself,' he went on. 'Maybe we could use them as a store. That old shed out there won't last much longer, I'll lay. What do you say to us going down there together?'

Susan and John were tremendously excited.

'Could we come too, Mr Doman? Please, Mr Doman, let us come.'

He smiled down at them. 'It's your mum and dad who'll have to say "yes" or "no" to that; but if your parents agree we'll make up a party and go exploring together. How about it, Vicar, and you, Mrs Exel?'

'You two go with the children. I'll stay at home.'

'No, that you won't, Mrs Exel. We can't have you moping in that huge vicarage all by yourself. Let's see, I haven't got much on tomorrow that the men can't see to. You come along at two o'clock. You, Mrs Exel, can keep my wife company. We'll go exploring, and be back for tea. You'll be very welcome. We're lonely up our end, and I hope you'll come.'

'Thank you, we will.'

'Good! Then that's settled. We'll be looking forward to it. Goodbye.' He hopped on his bicycle and pedalled away.

They took Belinda with them on Monday, and arrived at the farm punctually at two o'clock. Mr Doman was ready and waiting. They left Mummy with Mrs Doman, and put Belinda in a barn with Mr Doman's car for company.

'We won't go by the road,' said Mr Doman. 'We'll take the back way through the fields. That way Tipper won't see us coming. It's my belief he spends far more time at Blueton's than he does with my sheep, and I'm going to catch him out. Just a minute.' He unlocked a shed and selected a pick and shovel. 'We may not need these,' he said, 'but it's as well to have them in case.'

Thus armed they approached the field, and climbed over a hurdle blocking a gap in the hedge. They stood for a moment or two looking round.

'There!' said Mr Doman. 'What did I tell you?' Tipper came hurrying out of Mr Blueton's garden. They walked across, and by the time they

reached the steps leading to the cellar Tipper had sidled up behind.

'What were you doing over at Blueton's?'

'Just looking round, Mr Doman. Mr Blueton gets me to do a bit of digging at odd times.'

'Not in my time, he doesn't. I pay you to look after my sheep, not to dig Blueton's garden. Now take away these hurdles. We're going down.'

'Going down there, sir? Don't go. There's things down there – it's dangerous.'

'What things? Have you been down?'

'No, I dare not.'

'Why not?'

'Mr Blueton says it's dangerous.'

'How does he know?'

'He . . . He's been down, sir – him and some – friends of his.'

'Well, if that isn't calm, cool cheek. It's right what they say about him, the interfering beggar. Anyway, he seems to have come out safely, so why shouldn't we? Come on, shift those hurdles, Tipper.'

They crowded round the door. Daddy lifted the rusty catch and pushed. 'That's queer,' he said. 'The door was unlocked on Friday.'

'We'll soon settle that.' Mr Doman produced a bundle of keys from his pocket. 'I collect these things, you never know when they'll be useful.' They soon found one which opened the door.

Mr Doman was last in. He turned to Tipper. 'You stay here,' he ordered, 'and see that no one interferes with this door.'

'Yes, sir.'

'If we're not out by six o'clock, you'd better come in and find us. Else you'll likely have my wife down here, and you know what *that* means.'

Tipper did know; but he had his own way of dealing with it. He waited till Mr Doman had disappeared inside. Then he hurried over to Blueton's cottage, knocked, and went inside.

## 11 The secret passage

The first room the party entered was small and square. It had once been whitewashed, but was now mostly brick colour, and festooned with dirty cobwebs. To the right, an opening led into another room very like the first, but bigger. A pile of earth and rubble filled the middle of the opposite wall. Mr Doman pulled some of the rubbish away with his pick. 'Stone steps,' he said. 'That's where the stairs came down from the house most likely.' He shone his torch round the walls. 'Bricked up door there. Now what's this behind the stairs?' The beam of his torch had picked out a narrow opening.

'Surely this is new work?' said Daddy.

'By Jiminy, so it is!' agreed Mr Doman. 'Look

what's beyond.' They pushed through into a narrow passage whose walls were lined not with old brick, but with new concrete.

'This needs looking into.'

The passage was straight for about twenty metres, and then opened out into a long wide room. It was so long that the beams of their torches only faintly picked out the further end. Along the walls were wooden racks and shelves. The children ran on in front, shining their torches here, there, and everywhere, exclaiming at what they saw.

'Look, here's a cross. What's it doing here?'

'Here's another. It's silver with jewels on. There's candlesticks like we have in church at home.'

There were carpets and pictures on one side of the room; while silver and gold ornaments, mostly from churches, filled the racks on the other. Rolls of lead sheeting lay neatly on the floor.

'So that's what happened to our church roof,' said Mr Doman grimly.

'I shouldn't be surprised if ours wasn't here too,' said Daddy.

The children ran from pile to pile, calling to each other.

'Help! Help!'

'What's the matter, John?' queried his sister.

'I didn't call, Susan.'

'Someone called, and if it wasn't you, who was it?' asked Susan reasonably. 'Listen!' she said. 'There it is.'

The children ran back to the grown-ups. 'There's someone calling. We can hear him. There he is again.'

'Help! Help!'

'Let's go and see,' said Mr Doman, shouldering his pick. Daddy came behind with the shovel. The sound seemed to come from a small door in the far wall of the room.

'Who are you?'

'Bert Middley. Who are you?'

'It's Bert, it's Bert!' cried the children joyously. 'Bert, it's us, Susan and John and Daddy and Mr Doman.'

'Well, I never did,' said Mr Doman in wonderment. 'Fancy meeting a friend of yours shut down here. Come on, we'll get him out. Stand clear, children. Move away from behind that door, Bert,' and with his pick the farmer broke it down and set Bert free.

'How did you get down here, Bert?' asked Daddy.

'Jake brought me here to Mr Redgold. I was in a lorry wrapped up in a carpet. I've been down here since Thursday evening.'

The children were greatly excited, and quite

cock-a-hoop to find that they had been right about Bert being on the lorry and in a carpet; but Bert cut them short by asking:

'What day is it, please?'

'Monday. Why?'

'Gosh!' said Bert. 'We'll have to hurry. They're going to clear out tonight. I heard them say so.'

'Come on,' said Mr Doman. 'Back to the door.'

They rushed pell-mell to the little door, only to find it locked.

'Jiminy Christmas,' exclaimed Mr Doman. 'What a lot of fools we are. Look, they've even blocked up the keyhole.' Mr Doman's keys were useless.

'Now here's a business,' said Mr Doman. They took turns in battering the door with the pick; but it had been strengthened on the inside with steel plates, and the pick could make no impression.

Meanwhile the children had been shooed out of the way into the other room. 'Let's try and get up the stairs,' said Susan, so they borrowed the shovel, and using John's knife as well, they tried to clear away the rubbish. All they did was to break one of the blades of John's knife and bring down more rubbish. So they gave it up and looked elsewhere. John was disappointed about the stairs, he was also sad that he had broken his knife. He scratched with the broken blade at some bricks. The bricks were soft and crumbly, and the knife went in more deeply than he had expected. Presently he loosened a lump and pulled it out. There was a hole. 'Susan, let's have the torch a sec,' he called. He shone the torch on the place. There really was a hole right through the bricks. Susan looked too, then she ran back to the others.

'There's a place like a door,' she said, 'and it's got all bricks in it, and John's got a lump out with his knife, and there's a hole you can see through that there isn't anything the other side.'

Bert and Mr Doman looked puzzled; but Daddy understood. 'Come on,' he said. 'That sounds hopeful. Let's look.'

The bricks were old and soft and the mortar poor. A few stout blows with the pick made an opening through which Bert and John wriggled. They took a torch with them to explore. Their report was encouraging, and the hole was soon large enough for even Mr Doman to squeeze through.

The passage was brick lined. It turned and twisted. In places it was so filled with rubbish that they had to crawl; but at last they came to a dead end in a small oblong room. Some stone steps led up to the ceiling on one side, while a piece of rusty chain hung down from the other. A roughly shaped block of stone lay on the floor. It had a hole through which a piece of chain had been fastened.

'Perhaps there's a trap door,' Daddy said, looking at the steps. He climbed up and pushed at the ceiling. It moved a little. Mr Doman tried too, but with no better success.

Meanwhile Bert had been looking at the stone. He and John had a consultation. John lent him his knife, and after a long search in his pockets, produced a piece of string. Bert looped the string through the hole in the stone, then he asked Daddy to hold the stone up, while he tied the string to what was left of the hanging chain. The stone was heavy, and Daddy was glad when the last knot was tied, and the stone could hang free.

'Stand clear, children,' he ordered. 'Now try again, Mr Doman, please.'

Mr Doman pushed, the ceiling swung up easily. It was a slab pivoted in the middle. The end by the steps swung up, and the other end swung down into the little room. The stone balance weight made all the difference.

He stood on the top step, looking round. 'Well,

I'll be blowed,' he said, astonished. 'We're in the church.'

They crowded up and found they were standing under the tower. They lowered the stone slab gently. It was the tombstone they had looked at on Sunday morning. Daddy chuckled. 'There you are, Mr Doman,' he said. 'Your old vicar does move after all!'

## 12 Grand finale

Mr Doman's keys unlocked the door, and they peeped round the corner of the porch. They laughed to see two men on guard in the field; one at the door, and the other by the hut.

'I think there must be a way to the big room through the hut,' said Bert. 'I was blindfold when they brought me. It was dark too; but it felt as if they took me in there and let me down through a trap door.'

The two guards were bored. They sat down and chatted together. 'Now's our chance,' whispered Daddy. They hurried up the church path, and were soon safely at the farm. Only then did they notice the time. They were surprised. It was only a quarter past five. All the same there was no time to spare. While Bert and the children told their story to the two wondering ladies, Daddy and Mr Doman, tired as they were, couldn't relax.

Mr Doman telephoned the local police, who were most reluctant to believe anything against Mr Blueton. However, when Daddy rang Superintendent Sandson at Arlstead, and asked his help, things began to move. They barely had time to wash and finish their meal before Inspector Nailer arrived. They made plans together. The inspector called for reinforcements, and by half-past-six they were ready to start.

Meanwhile there was another conference. This one was in Blueton's house. Mr Blueton was having difficulty. Spike and Jake were nervous. They wanted to run away at once.

'Don't be in such a hurry.'

'But, Bandmaster, we've got to. Tipper was a fool. He should have jammed the door, so that they couldn't get in. He locked them in instead. They'll be missed – especially the children. There'll be a hue and cry any minute.'

'Exactly, Jake. That is just why we aren't going. We must wait till it starts.'

'Sounds daft,' muttered the two men rebelliously.

'It's common sense. Farmer told Tipper they were expected back at six. Mrs Doman will wait –

say half an hour. Her husband's often late, and she won't want the constable to think her an anxious fool, calling him out for nothing. As I said, she'll wait half an hour, and then call the police. The constable will take some time to arrive – say ten minutes – so we can expect them here at a quarter to seven.

'The constable, worthy man, knows me as a respectable resident. He'll come here and inquire. I shall say that I saw the party leave the field and go to the woods. We'll then call Tipper. Tipper'll say that they did try to go down the cellars but couldn't open the door, so they went to the woods instead.

'We'll go across the field and show the constable the door, convincingly battered by Tipper, as evidence. He and others in the search party'll go and beat the woods. The coast'll be clear and we can leave with no one to see us.'

Jake was still not convinced, and said so.

'Hasty action, my dear Jake, always brings trouble. It's your greatest fault.'

The door burst open. Tipper and the other guard tumbled into the room. 'They're out,' they panted. 'It's a raid. Scram!'

'Control yourself, Tipper. Who and what do you mean?'

'The parson and the farmer. They've brought police. They're in the field now.'

Mr Blueton forgot his principles. He took very hasty action. In one bound he was at the door. Elbowing the other men aside, he made for the barn. Jake followed hard behind. The two men struggled for the lorry's controls. Blueton won. The other three just managed to grab hold and pull themselves in, before it started. There was no time to open the doors. The lorry charged them. They burst outwards like matchwood. Blueton guessed the police had blocked Church Lane. He wrenched the wheel sharp left, and drove at a jolting, reckless speed over Farmer

Doman's rough grass fields. Gates collapsed in splinters. He swung left again to the trackway of the ancient road. 'The other road'll be blocked both at village and farm,' he thought swiftly. 'This track's our only chance.'

There were gates each side where the track crossed the road. The lorry bounced over pot-holes, crashed through both gates and began to storm the hill. 'They forgot this way out,' he chortled. 'I've diddled them again.'

When kind Mrs Doman had heard Bert's story, she couldn't do enough for him. She bustled about, got a bath ready for him, found him clean clothes, and gave him more food for tea than he could eat. He wanted to help in rounding up the Band; but the police thought that would be unwise. Bert was disappointed. 'Is there any place here,' he asked, 'from which I could watch everything?'

Mrs Doman thought for a moment. 'I know the very place,' she smiled, and took him to the front door. She pointed to the woods on the hill top. 'You see that break in the trees. That's where an old road goes. It's only a track now; but the Vicar says the Romans made it, and it was important when the village was round the church. Nobody uses it but us. We find it handy, getting to our top fields. I've been there often. I love it. You can see the whole valley from there.'

'Thanks, Mrs Doman,' said Bert. 'That sounds just the job. I'll go up now.' The children asked if they could go too. Mummy was doubtful, but when Bert promised to take great care, and Mrs Doman explained that the place was right out of the way, Mummy allowed herself to be persuaded. She said that Bert could drive them there in Belinda.

On the way they all told Belinda about their adventures, and when they reached the top, Bert turned Belinda round, and parked her on the slope where the track entered the trees. Then all three got out and settled down to watch.

They saw Daddy and two policemen go to the church. 'They're going down our secret passage, I expect,' they said to themselves. The two guards raced to the house. Then Mr Doman and three policemen reached the field. Other police surrounded the house. When the two guards burst in, these closed in too. 'They've got them,' cried the children. 'It's all over.'

'No, it isn't then!' cried Bert suddenly. The barn door exploded outwards, and the lorry careered across the fields. The children bounced with excitement as police rushed back to head it off at the road.

'Gosh!' exclaimed Bert. 'Look at that! They're coming up here.' The lorry crashed the gates and began to climb the track. Bert was worried about the children. Not without difficulty, he made them go out of sight among the trees. Then he ran back to move Belinda. He stood stock-still in horror. Belinda had gone.

While the others sat on the grass, Belinda enjoyed the evening sun. She hadn't liked climbing the steep, rough track; but it was nice here, and she basked in the pleasant warmth. While she basked, she thought. She thought about lorries and ditches, she thought about Bert and carpets. She was still rather muddled, and believed that the lorry had rolled Bert in a carpet. That made her very cross.

'What a dreadful thing to do,' she said to herself. 'Rolling Bert in a carpet is almost as bad as rolling *me* in a ditch. That lorry needs a sharp lesson. If ever I see it again I'll – I'll – I don't know what I'll do.'

'Gosh! Look at that! They're coming up here.'

Bert's exclamation roused Belinda from her thoughts. She could scarcely believe it, but there, at the bottom of the hill, looking so small that it might have been an insect, was – that lorry.

'Well for evermore!' she said. 'The cheek of it. That lorry's coming up here to catch my Bert and roll him in a carpet again. Shouldn't be surprised if he wants to roll Susan and John too. What a dreadful thing! What shall I do?'

Then suddenly Belinda knew what she must do.

She felt a little frightened, for the lorry was big, and she was small. Then she thought about Susan and John, and felt brave again. She shook herself in her own special way. Her hand-brake slipped, as she knew it would. She began to roll gently down the hill. The ruts kept her wheels on the track. That was lucky for Belinda, otherwise she would soon have been in the ditch. It was lucky too that the road was rough, because it kept her from going too fast: that would have been dangerous. As it was, she rolled down bumpily, but with dignity, rather like an old mother duck taking a walk.

Two months ago, at haytime, Mr Doman had had to halt one of his carts on the way up the hill. He had wedged a large stone in a rut to keep the cart from going back. That stone still lay in the roadway. Belinda stopped with a gentle bump. 'Bother it,' she said crossly. 'I was just beginning to go faster too.' She could hear the lorry roaring up the steepest part of the hill; but she couldn't see it. She felt helpless and a little frightened. She wished Mr Exel or Bert were here. Bert was panting down the hill behind.

The lorry was coming up fast in front. Jake and Blueton were in the driving cab. They were on top of the world, quite sure they had outwitted

the police, and were away on a clear, unguarded road. They topped the steepest rise. Jake saw Belinda first. 'Confound it!' he yelled. 'That pesky little car again! Swing left, you fool, left,' and stupidly he grabbed the steering wheel. For a few seconds he and Blueton struggled for the wheel, and those few seconds killed their chances of escape. The lorry swung wildly from side to side. Its front wheel caught in the ditch, and it rolled helplessly into the hedge.

Belinda, surprised and relieved to find herself unhurt, surveyed it with satisfaction. 'It just serves you right, you silly great lorry,' she said severely. 'That'll teach you to roll my Bert in carpets.'

Bert and the police arrived as the Band struggled out of the lorry. They were dazed and easily rounded up. Bert drove Belinda to the top to collect the children. 'You're a very naughty little car,' he said crossly. 'Running down the hill like that.'

'But, Bert,' sobbed Belinda, much hurt, 'I w – w – w – wanted to s – s – stop that l – l – lorry.'

'To stop that lorry?' said Bert, amazed.

'Y – Y – Yes, Bert. I w – w – wanted to st – stop it catching you and Susan and John and rolling you in carpets. And I did too.'

'So that was it,' said Bert thoughtfully. 'I'm sorry I was cross, Belinda. I think you're very brave. You might have been hurt.'

'Yes, Bert. I'm glad I wasn't.'

'So am I,' said Bert, with feeling.

They drove to the farm, and when Daddy and Mr Doman arrived, Mummy and the children were transferred to the vicarage, while the three men went to the police-station. Bert told them everything he knew about the Band. The inspector thanked him but gave him a dressing down too.

'You're not to blame,' he said, 'for joining the Band, because you didn't know what they were doing. You did right to leave them, but you did wrong in not telling the police at Arlstead. If you had done that, you'd have saved us all a great deal of trouble. It's silly to be frightened of us. We policemen are here to help and protect all honest people.'

Bert stayed with the vicarage family for a week. Then he went back to Arlstead, where George Egg and William Whisker were very glad to see him. He now helps George in the repair shop, and is very happy. He was happier still, when, a short while ago, he found a little house nearby, in which he and his mother and brother and sister now live.

The arrest of the Band caused a sensation. The papers were full of it for a few days, and the vicarage family were pestered by reporters. They got very tired of it. Not so Belinda; she enjoyed being photographed, and a great many pictures were taken of her. The one she liked best showed her standing on the old track with the lorry nearby, on its side, in the ditch. Mr Exel very kindly bought a copy for her, and it now hangs framed in her garage at Arlstead. She is very proud of it and never gets tired of showing it to visitors.

'There,' she says proudly. 'That's my photograph, that is. Me, and my Jewel and all. That old lorry in the ditch, that's the Band. Must be, 'cos Susan says I beat it. Look, she wrote letters underneath all about it. Can you read them? I can, 'cos Susan told me what they are. Shall I read them to you? I think I'd better. You mightn't be able to read them properly like me. The letters say: BELINDA BEATS THE BAND. What d'you think of that?'

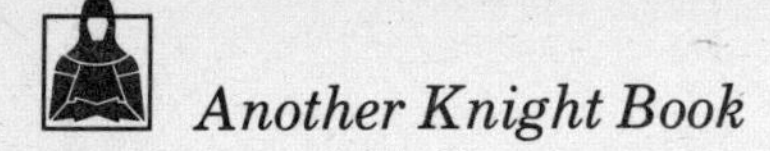


*Rev W Awdry*

BELINDA THE BEETLE

Belinda is a little red Volkswagen Beetle and as soon as Susan and John and their parents see her in William Whisker's garage, they know that she's the only car for them. But a gang of thieves is interested in the little car too – what can they be after?

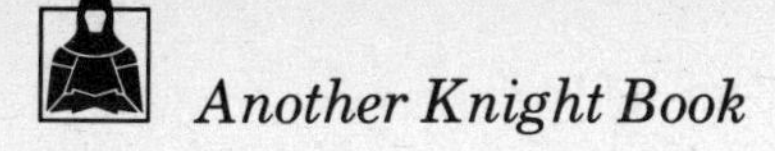

*Another Knight Book*

*Rolf Harris*

YOUR CARTOON TIME

Did you know that you can draw?

Rolf Harris shows you how – clearly and simply – in YOUR CARTOON TIME. Starting with stick figures, he explains how to develop these step-by-step into your own stylish characters, and there are ideas too for how you can use your drawings – as birthday cards, home movies and so on.

Drawing is fun!

All you need is a pencil, paper and Rolf Harris's book – YOUR CARTOON TIME.

*A complete list of the* FAMOUS FIVE ADVENTURES *by Enid Blyton*

---

1 FIVE ON A TREASURE ISLAND
2 FIVE GO ADVENTURING AGAIN
3 FIVE RUN AWAY TOGETHER
4 FIVE GO TO SMUGGLER'S TOP
5 FIVE GO OFF IN A CARAVAN
6 FIVE ON KIRRIN ISLAND AGAIN
7 FIVE GO OFF TO CAMP
8 FIVE GET INTO TROUBLE
9 FIVE FALL INTO ADVENTURE
10 FIVE ON A HIKE TOGETHER
11 FIVE HAVE A WONDERFUL TIME
12 FIVE GO DOWN TO THE SEA
13 FIVE GO TO MYSTERY MOOR
14 FIVE HAVE PLENTY OF FUN
15 FIVE ON A SECRET TRAIL
16 FIVE GO TO BILLYCOCK HILL
17 FIVE GET INTO A FIX
18 FIVE ON FINNISTON FARM
19 FIVE GO TO DEMON'S ROCKS
20 FIVE HAVE A MYSTERY TO SOLVE
21 FIVE ARE TOGETHER AGAIN

Have you played any of these exciting
Hodder & Stoughton Adventure Game books?